The Poisoned Apple

A Fractured Fairy Tale

To my unfailingly patient and supportive husband.

Copyright © 2020 Anne Lambelet. First published in 2020 by Page Street Kids, an imprint of Page Street Publishing Co., 27 Congress Street, Suite 105, Salem, MA 01970. www.pagestreetpublishing.com. All rights reserved. No part of this book may be reproduced or used, in any form or by any means, electronic or mechanical, without prior permission in writing from the publisher. Distributed by Macmillan, sales in Canada by The Canadian Manda Group. ISBN-13: 978-1-64567-060-5. ISBN-10: 1-64567-060-0. CIP data for this book is available from the Library of Congress. This book was typeset in Adobe Garamond Pro. The illustrations were done digitally. Printed and bound in Shenzhen, Guangdong, China.
20 21 22 23 24 CCO 5 4 3 2 1

Page Street Publishing uses only materials from suppliers who are committed to responsible and sustainable forest management. Page Street Publishing protects our planet by donating to nonprofits like The Trustees, which focuses on local land conservation.

The Poisoned Apple

A FRACTURED FAIRY TALE

Anne Lambelet

PAGE STREET KIDS

Once there was a witch who detested a princess. This particular princess was getting a little too sweet for her own good, and any decent witch knows just how to deal with a princess like that:

a poisoned apple.

For months and months, the witch had worked tirelessly to collect countless rare ingredients. She had only enough for a single apple-poisoning spell, so everything would have to go exactly according to plan.

First, she mixed the ingredients in her cauldron. Next, she carefully dipped the apple into the bubbling brew. It began to transform.

The spell had worked!

Her secret weapon now complete, the witch waited for
the princess to pass through the woods . . .

and gave her

the poisoned apple.

The witch's plot was in motion! Now she'd get to watch from the woods as the princess took her final bite.

The princess had been on her way to the dwarfs' diamond mine to bring them lunch.

The witch watched impatiently as the princess handed out provisions to the hungry men. To the sixth dwarf she gave

The poisoned apple.

After polishing off most of his other food, the sixth dwarf
started to take a bite . . .

when he was interrupted by a couple of hungry forest animals.

Since he was already pretty full, he supposed he could share.

So, he gave them

The Poisoned Apple.

Happily, the animals leaned in to take a bite . . .

when they were startled by a foraging squirrel, desperate for something to feed her babies.

Their hearts went out to the hungry little ones,
so they gave her

The poisoned apple.

The witch couldn't let the apple get away!
She hadn't put all that work in for nothing.

She had no choice but to climb, climb, climb
right up that tree after the squirrel.

She had only a little farther to go, when suddenly . . .

CRACK!

Down . . . .

down . . . .

down . . . .

the witch   fell.

When she came to, she couldn't remember who she was, where she was, or what she'd been doing. The squirrel was concerned and gave her a tasty-looking apple.

It seemed strangely familiar, but the witch was hungry. . . .

And so, having unwittingly escaped the witch's scheme, everyone in the forest lived happily ever after.

Well...

almost everyone.